the **BAD GUYS**

in

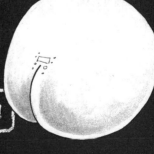

THE OTHERS?!

TEXT AND ILLUSTRATIONS COPYRIGHT © 2022 BY AARON BLABEY

ALL RIGHTS RESERVED. PUBLISHED BY SCHOLASTIC PRESS, AN IMPRINT OF
SCHOLASTIC INC., PUBLISHERS SINCE 1920. SCHOLASTIC AND ASSOCIATED LOGOS ARE
TRADEMARKS AND/OR REGISTERED TRADEMARKS OF SCHOLASTIC INC. THIS EDITION
PUBLISHED UNDER LICENSE FROM SCHOLASTIC AUSTRALIA PTY LIMITED. FIRST
PUBLISHED BY SCHOLASTIC AUSTRALIA PTY LIMITED IN 2015.

THE PUBLISHER DOES NOT HAVE ANY CONTROL OVER AND DOES NOT ASSUME ANY
RESPONSIBILITY FOR AUTHOR OR THIRD-PARTY WEBSITES OR THEIR CONTENT.

NO PART OF THIS PUBLICATION MAY BE REPRODUCED, STORED IN A RETRIEVAL SYSTEM,
OR TRANSMITTED IN ANY FORM OR BY ANY MEANS, ELECTRONIC, MECHANICAL,
PHOTOCOPYING, RECORDING, OR OTHERWISE, WITHOUT WRITTEN PERMISSION OF
THE PUBLISHER. FOR INFORMATION REGARDING PERMISSION, WRITE TO SCHOLASTIC
AUSTRALIA, AN IMPRINT OF SCHOLASTIC AUSTRALIA PTY LIMITED,
345 PACIFIC HIGHWAY, LINDFIELD NSW 2070 AUSTRALIA.

THIS BOOK IS A WORK OF FICTION. NAMES, CHARACTERS, PLACES, AND INCIDENTS ARE
EITHER THE PRODUCT OF THE AUTHOR'S IMAGINATION OR ARE USED FICTITIOUSLY, AND ANY
RESEMBLANCE TO ACTUAL PERSONS, LIVING OR DEAD, BUSINESS ESTABLISHMENTS, EVENTS, OR
LOCALES IS ENTIRELY COINCIDENTAL.

ISBN 978-1-338-82053-9

1 2022

PRINTED IN THE U.S.A.   23
FIRST U.S. PRINTING 2022

· AARON BLABEY ·

the BAD GUYS

in

THE OTHERS?!

gzzzt!

gzzzt!

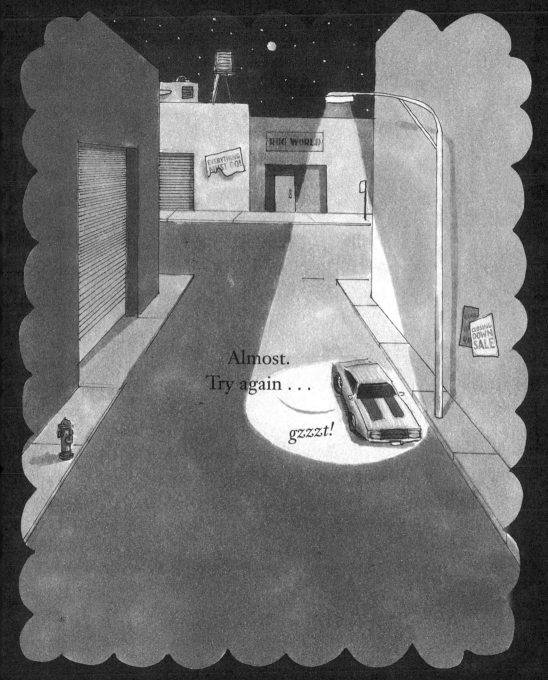

Yes, sir.
Thank you, sir . . .

CHAPTER 1

THE REALLY BAD LADY

ACK!

I have made some
**POOR
DECISIONS**
in my life.
But coming here just
about takes the cake.

GAAARRRRRGH!

OK.
I'm afraid I need to talk to ABE,
so get ready—take your hand
away on three . . .

One . . .

two . . .

three!

gasp!

GAAARRGGH! WHAT IS WRONG WITH YOU?!

Wolfie! *Chill.*

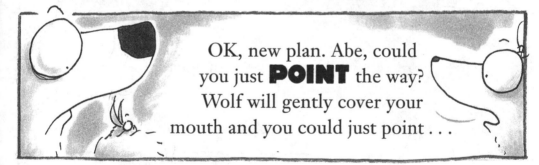

OK, new plan. Abe, could you just **POINT** the way? Wolf will gently cover your mouth and you could just point . . .

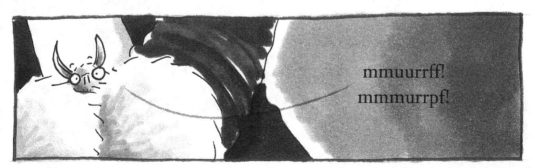

mmuurrff! mmmurrpf!

What's that?
I don't understand.

mmuurrff!

Wolfie, let him speak . . .

I can definitely point!
That's a great idea.
*But there's something
I need to tell
you first . . .*

SNIFF SNIFF

She didn't see us!

Wolfie . . .
YOUR HAIR!

Gah!
Yours too!

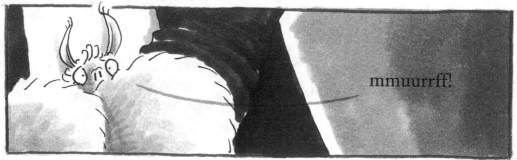

mmuurrff!

It's HER.
She's so *bad* that
she creates
**BAD LUCK,
BAD WEATHER,
BAD MOODS,**
and **BAD HAIR.**

Bad moods?
Come to think of it . . .
maybe that's why I feel so
GROUCHY . . .

· CHAPTER 2 ·
FORWARD OR BACK?

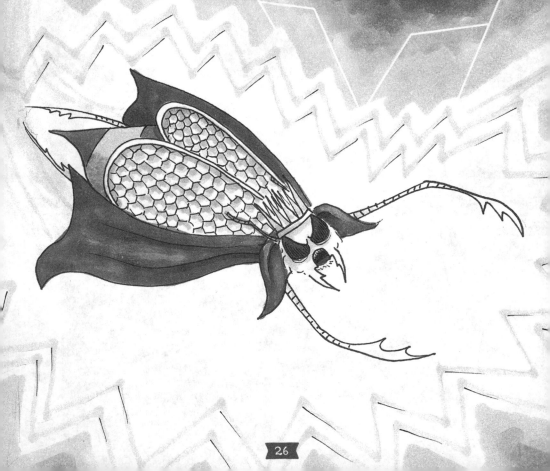

I agree! This is
SHAMEFUL!
Mr. Piranha has *never*
run away from a fight!

Are you sure you
can't protect **ALL**
of us with . . .

. . . with . . .

. . . with?

YOUR **MAGIC BUTT?**

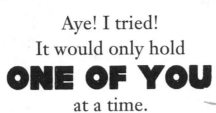

Aye! I tried!
It would only hold
ONE OF YOU
at a time.

WHY?!

I don't know.

That's it.
I'm turning us around.
I'm not leaving
SHARK,
and I'm not leaving
HOGWILD.
There has to be a way . . .

YEAH!
LET'S DO THAT!

Wait!
What about **AGENT FOX?**
Doesn't she need me?

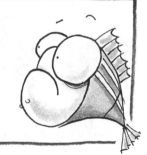

She can't find the
DOORWAYS
without you . . .

This is a nightmare.

WHAT ARE WE GOING TO DO?!

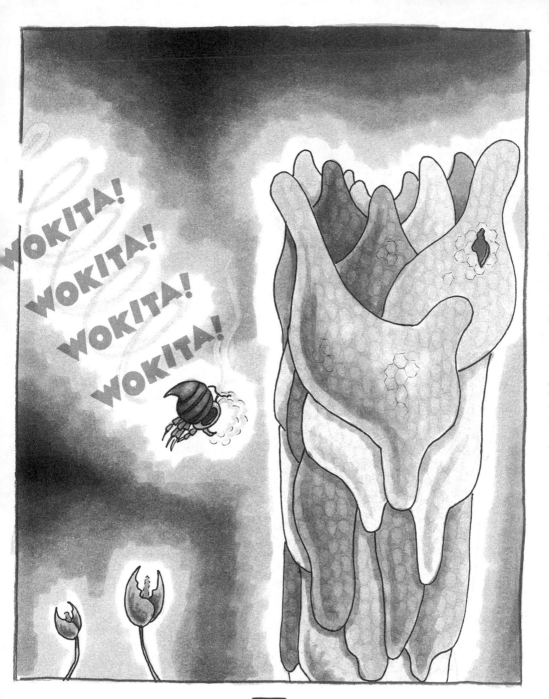

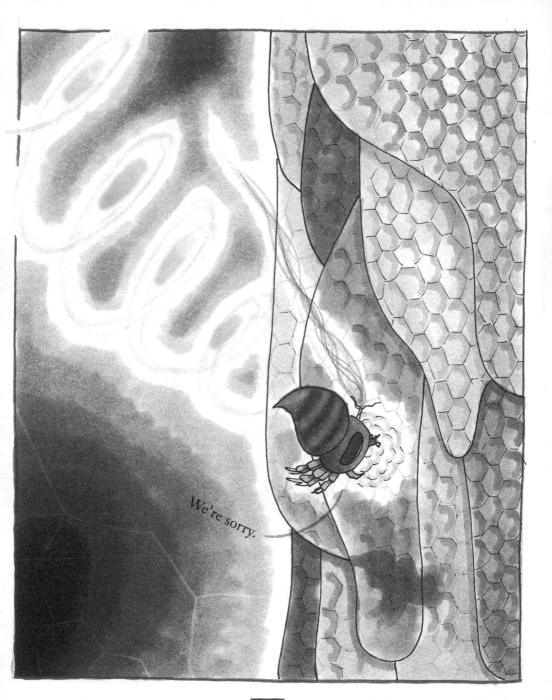

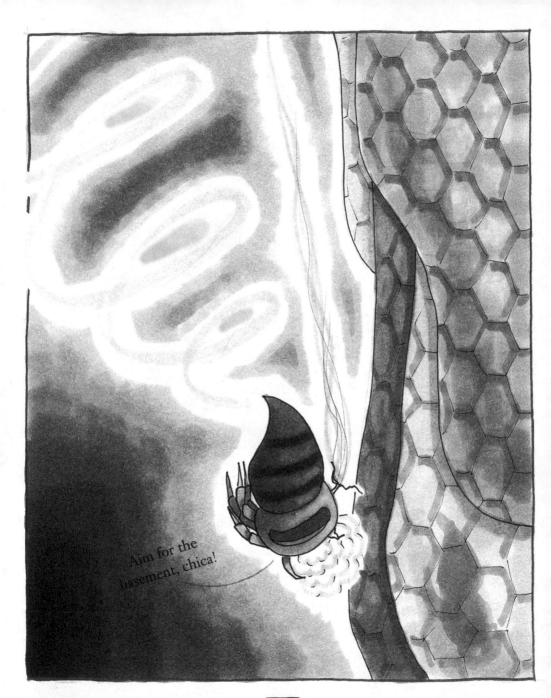

· CHAPTER 3 ·
BULL

Why on earth didn't you tell us, Mr. Thunders? Was it some kind of **TEST?**

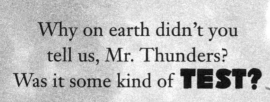

YEAH . . .

Well, I think we can safely say that *I* am the only one who passed the test, right, Buck?

YEAH!

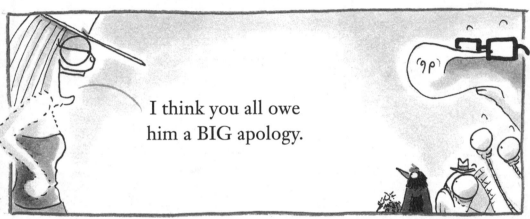

I think you all owe
him a BIG apology.

Wait a minute . . .

I DON'T TRUST BUCK

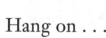

He's certainly very **CONFIDENT.**

That's right!
And what more does
a leader need than
CONFIDENCE?

I don't know,
INTELLIGENCE, maybe?

WISDOM . . .

INTEGRITY,
COMPASSION,
PEOPLE SKILLS,
TRUSTWORTHINESS . . .

And he has both of those things, right?

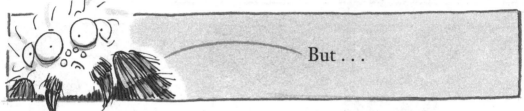

But . . .

Nuh-uh-uh.
I don't want to hear it.
ALL
I want to hear from this ragtag menagerie of wiggly, flappy, slimy little
ODDBODS
is that
YOU WERE WRONG . . .

I WAS RIGHT . . .

and BUCK THUNDERS is the **HERO** we've been waiting for.

I mean, **LOOK AT HIM!** *How did you not see it?!* OF COURSE he's one of **THE OTHERS.**

Sorry . . .
who is this guy?

Hold that
thought . . .

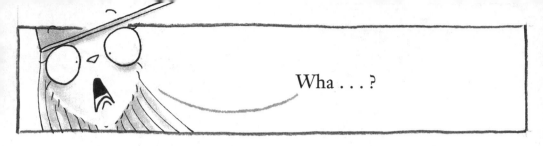

Wha . . . ?

You thought that **BUBBLEHEAD** was one of The Others? What's wrong with you, gal?

But . . .

Good grief! If he's not one of The Others, *who is he*?

WE HAVE TO STOP HIM!

A SPY?!

LET'S GO!

A SPY?!

· CHAPTER 4 ·
THE THING

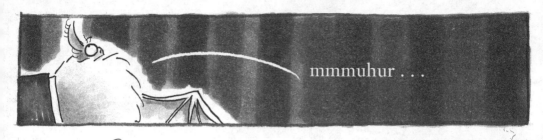

mmmuhur . . .

Yes? No?
Is this the way
or not?

Yes, but I really have to
tell you something . . .

Zip it, Mr. Honesty.
Tell me later,
once we get there.

If I had to guess . . .

I'd say this is the place.

Looks deserted.

A stroke of **GOOD LUCK,** wouldn't you say?

Ummm . . .

HIYA!

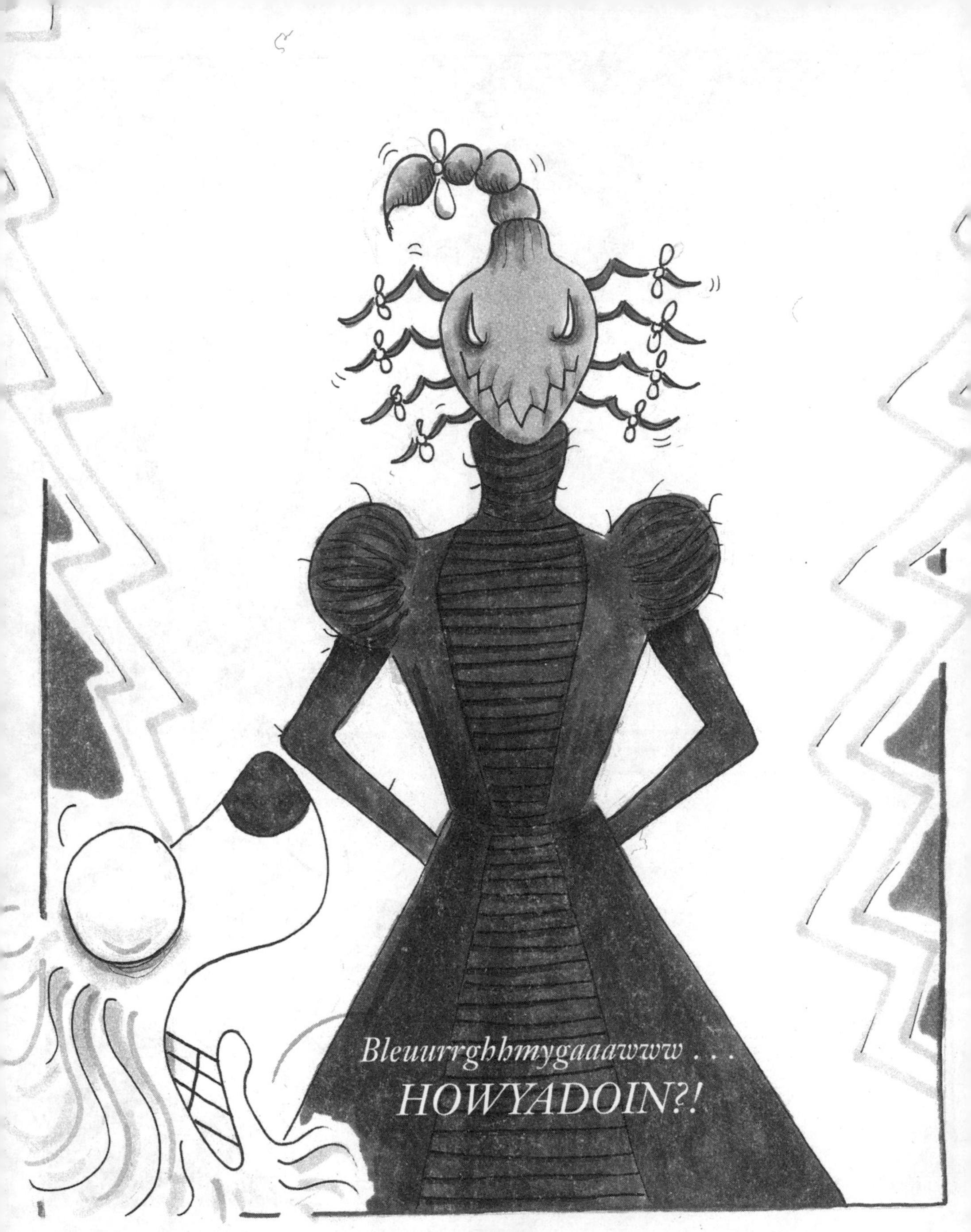
Bleuurrghhmygaaawww . . .
HOWYADOIN?!

Oh-kay doh-kay . . .

We mean you no harm!
Yaknowwhaddimsayin'?
We are merely . . . weary travelers,
passing through your . . .

beautiful land . . .

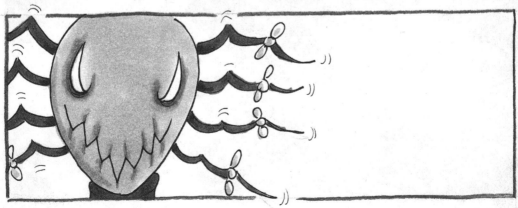

Oooh!
What's *THIS*?

How *thoughtful.*
Oh, you *shouldn't* have . . .

WINK!

I *really* need to tell you something . . .

Shhh!
Hmmm, whatever could this *be*?

What do you need to tell him?

Well, I was going to tell him that this is **UNDERLORD ESMERALDA GHASTLY, MOTHER OF NIGHT TERRORS.** I was also going to tell him that she carries a little **ORNATE BOX.** What's more, I was going to tell him that inside that little box is the **MOST FRIGHTENING THING IN THE ENTIRE MULTIVERSE,** and if you **LOOK AT IT,** you . . .

INSTANTLY DIE OF FRIGHT.

Do you think I should interrupt and mention it?

· CHAPTER 5 ·
WHISTLE STOP

I should warn you, señorita, I get **MOTION SICKNESS...**

YOU **FART,** YOU **DIE,** *GOT IT?*

I understand.

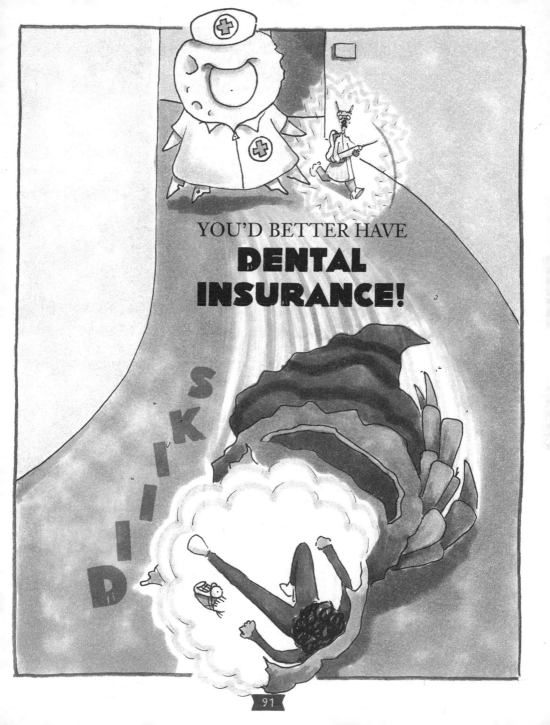

AAAAR
GGRR
HHH!

· CHAPTER 6 ·
FINALLY, A FEW ANSWERS

Someone has had their **ILLUSIONS SHATTERED.** This will not be pretty.

We'd better skedaddle, groovers.

OK, no.
I'm not going ANYWHERE
until I get some
ANSWERS.

I WAS RIGHT
ABOUT

Hiiii-YA!

Whoa.

Answers to what, birdie?

WHO *ARE* YOU GUYS?!

WHO *ARE*
THE OTHERS
EXACTLY?

Has no one told you?

NO!

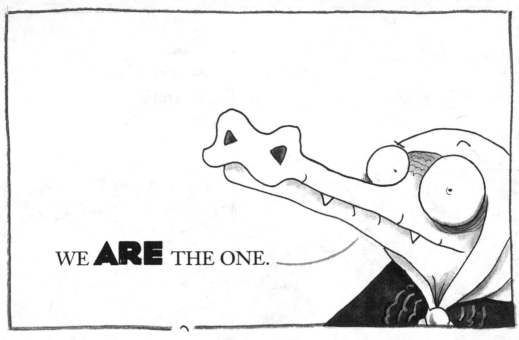

WE **ARE** THE ONE.

What she means is—
We are

PARTS

of THE ONE.

Dig this—

A LOOOOOOOOOOOOONG time ago,

THE ONE

SPLIT HERSELF INTO PARTS

so that the centipede couldn't

get her . . .

She **HID** those parts of herself

AROUND THE MULTIVERSE

to **PROTECT** herself from the centipede.

She **HID THOSE PARTS**

until she was ready to *face him*.

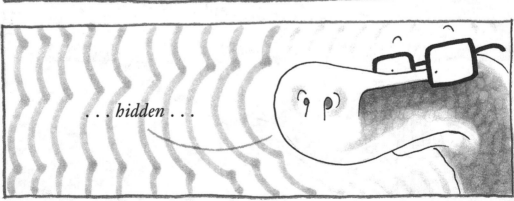

. . . hidden . . .

WE . . . **ARE** THOSE PARTS. And she's not complete without us.

But NOW it's time for her to face him, so we need to get back to THE ONE . . .

It's time for us to **COMPLETE HER.**

And when you
say "WE," you mean
YOU,
a really old alligator,
and **HIM,**
the weird little guy,
with the hair.

That's kind of rude . . .

What? He's got a
MULLET.
We're all thinking it.

It looks good on *him*.

Does it, though?

Hey, we may not
be much to look at,
but when combined
with THE ONE . . .

WE ARE
THE
ULTIMATE
FORCE
FOR GOOD.

. . . *good* . . .

But how does it work? Do you just hold hands with THE ONE and she's "complete" again?

Not quite, missy. Close, but not quite.

We'll explain on the way. You need to get us there **BEFORE IT'S TOO LATE.**

Without us,
THE ONE WILL FAIL.

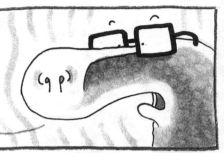

. . . *without us,*
The One will fail . . .

Are you OK, Milt?
You're acting
kind of weird . . .

CRASH!

Fluffit! Have you gotten it out of your system?

WE NEED TO GO!

YOU'RE A SPY?!

I guess not . . .

· CHAPTER 7 ·
OVER AND OUT

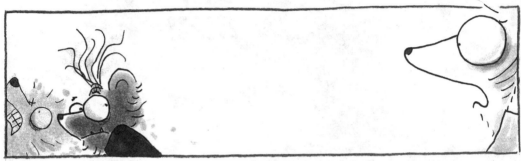

NOOOOO!

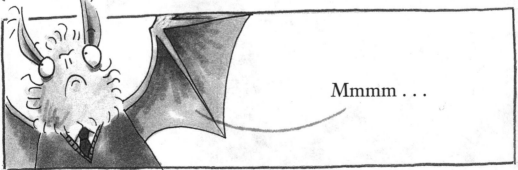

Mmmm . . .

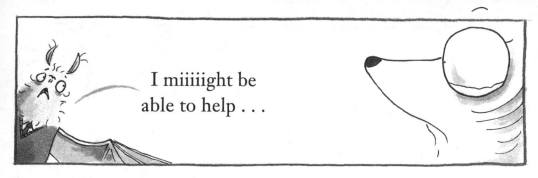

I miiiiight be able to help . . .

REALLY?! PLEASE! PLEASE HELP HIM!

I really should be getting back to the HOSPITAL, though.
I need to wait for THE ONE.

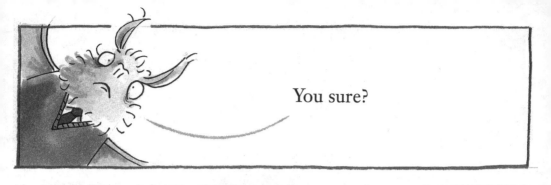

You sure?

Yes, yes,
I'm The One.
And you said that
you're one of
The Others, right?
**AREN'T
THE OTHERS
SUPPOSED
TO HELP ME?**

Well, I guess if you *are*
The One . . .

He is kind of dead, though . . .

PLEASE!

OK.
I'll give it a try.

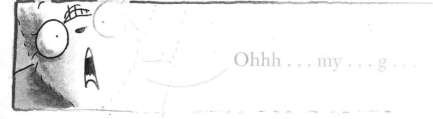

Wolfie?

Fox?

CRASH!

WHERE'S THE DOORWAY?!

UNDER THE RUG!

Remind me why we're bringing this lunatic?

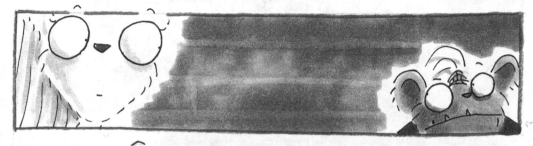

He has his moments . . .

GAAARGH!

We have to jump into **THAT?!** That's impossible!

He wants us to *think* it's impossible.

We just have to **BELIEVE** it's not.

It's a **LEAP OF FAITH.**

HUP!

Ellen!

Wait for me!

Are you *sure*
she's The One?

GRAB!

THUD!

· CHAPTER 8 ·
TIFFANY'S EPIPHANY

SUCCESS!

GOOD LOOKS!

LUXURY BRANDS!

LIFE WAS SIMPLE. **I KNEW WHO I WAS.**

Fluffit?

HE'S NOT A HERO, IS HE?

No, but we kind of have more important things to deal with right now.

NO, YOU'RE NOT A HERO . . .

YOU'RE JUST A COWARDLY LITTLE SPY.

A FAKE!

A PHONEY!

Fluffit, you're at a 10. We need you at a 2.

DID YOU SAY "FLUFFIT"?!

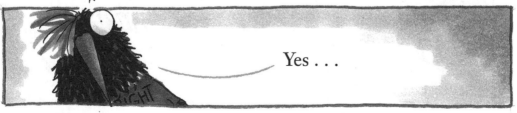

Yes . . .

I'm not sure I do . . .

I'M A PHONEY, TOO!
I'M NO BETTER THAN THIS GUY!

I WAS RIGHT ABOUT BUCK

MY REAL NAME ISN'T **TIFFANY FLUFFIT!** I MEAN, WHO'S NAMED **TIFFANY FLUFFIT?!** SERIOUSLY?!

SNAP!

That's just a **STAGE NAME.** I changed it when I got my first job on TV.

DELORES GRISTLEWURST!

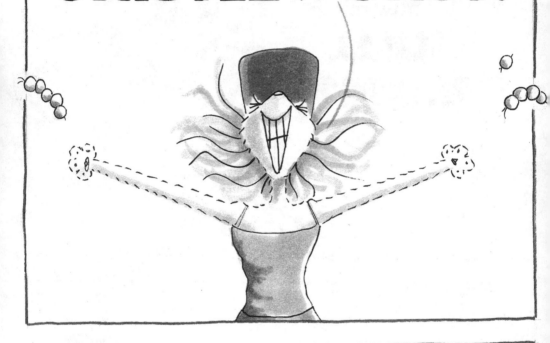

I WAS RIGHT ABOUT

Your name is
Delores Gristlewurst?

YES, IT IS!

And you know what?

I'm **PROUD** to be DELORES GRISTLEWURST

because DELORES GRISTLEWURST is **REAL!**

DELORES GRISTLEWURST is **NOT A FAKE!**

And DELORES GRISTLEWURST could spot a

PHONEY like **THAT GUY** from a **MILE AWAY!**

She's snapped . . .

DELORES GRISTLEWURST

is the HERO of this story.

AND SO ARE **YOU!**
WE ARE **ALL THE HEROES** OF
THIS STORY.

I kind of like Delores Gristlewurst.

Ditto.

AND
THIS
ONE!

AND . . .
Wait . . .
didn't you say
there's another
Other here?

If it's not
Buck Thunders . . .
WHO
IS IT?

Uh . . . I know this might sound a little odd . . .

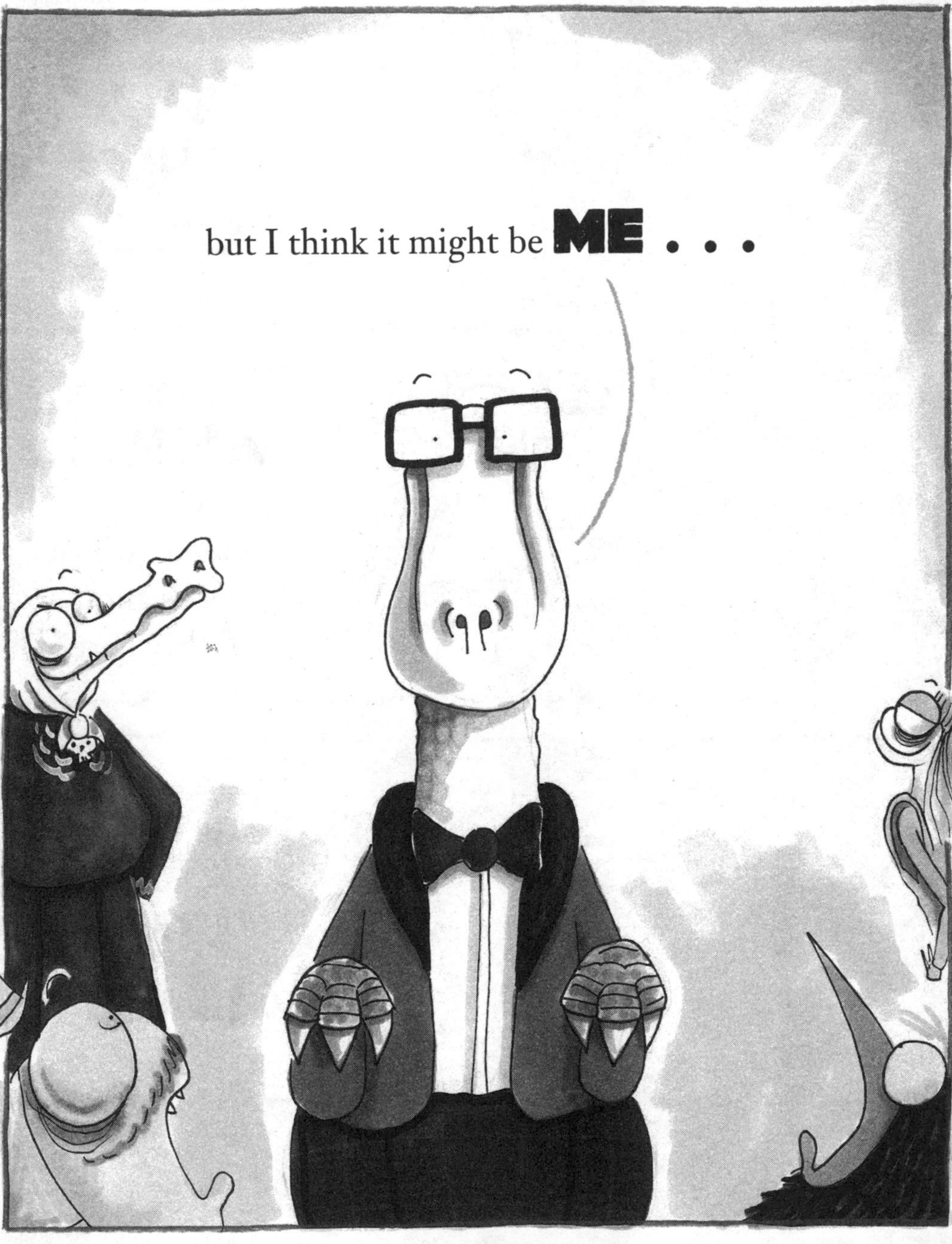
but I think it might be **ME** . . .

· CHAPTER 9 ·
A TERRIBLE SHOCK

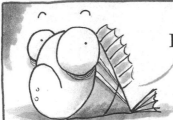

I need a minute,
por favor . . .

For what?

I need to poop.

I TOLD YOU—
I GET MOTION SICKNESS!

And did I **FART?**

NO.

But now?

NOW I NEED TO POOP.

Eight years of med school, for this . . .

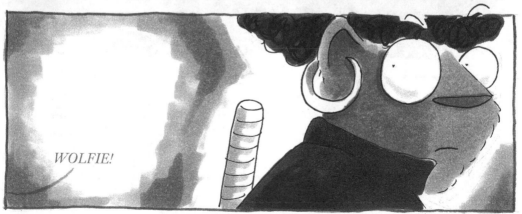

WOLFIE!

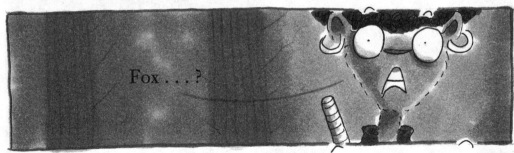

Hey, PIRANHA!
SHUT IT DOWN!
I JUST FOUND
**FOXY AND
THE GUYS!**

Piranha?

Where the . . . ?

Or BUTTER KNIFE.
Whatever you want
to call it.

I've always **ADMIRED** that about you.

And I'm not the only one . . .

HI, KITTY!
DUGGA DUGGA DUGGA DUGGA DUGGA DUGGA DUGGA DUGGA DUGGA DUGGA DUGGA DUGGA DUGGA DUGGA DUGGA DUGGA DUGGA DUGGA DUGGA
HI, KITTY KITTY KITTY!
Shark?!

· CHAPTER 10 ·
IN NO WAY GOOD

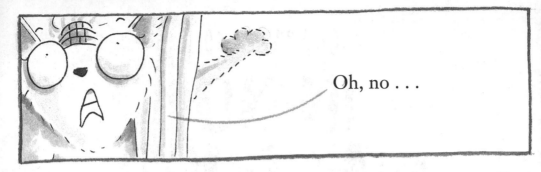

Oh, no . . .

SMACK!

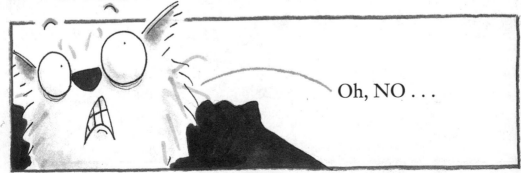

Oh, NO . . .

Oh, yeah . . .

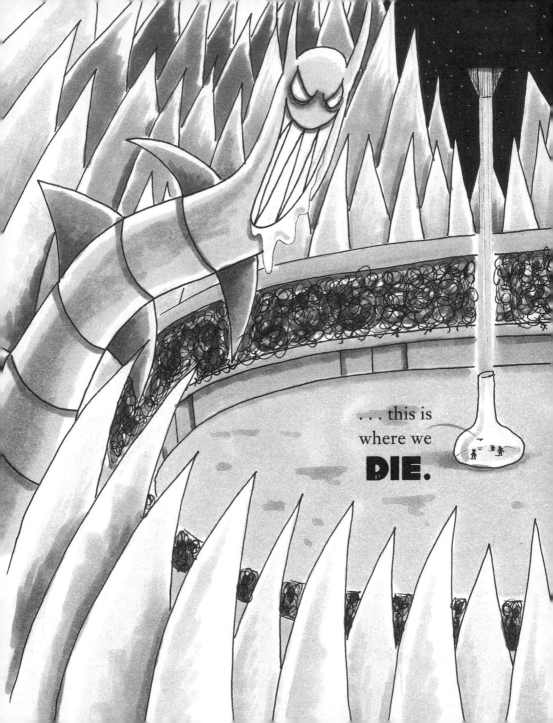

TO BE CONTINUED . . .

OK.

It's time to stop messin' around . . .

In the **VERY NEXT** installment:

The One **IS** going to be reunited with The Others.

You **ARE** going to actually meet the **REAL**

DREAD OVERLORD SPLAARGHÖN

and **ONE CHARACTER** is going to change

EVERYTHING

you thought you knew.

This is the one you've been waiting for . . .

the **BAD GUYS** BOOK **17**
COMING SOON!